Illustrated by Olga Zhuravlova

Additional graphics: 0melapics, SilviaNatalia, Vectorpocket/Freepik

Mat Waugh

www.matwaugh.co.uk

Produced by Big Red Button Books, a division of Say So Media Ltd.

ISBN: 978-1-912883-06-6

First published: March 2015

This edition: December 2018

MAT WAUGH

For Doris, Isla and Kirsty. I love it when you laugh in the right places.

And for Kate, who makes everything possible.

MY STORIES

A message from me

*Thanks for coming. Are you sitting comfortably?
Are there any toy diggers poking into your bottom?
Any weird itches or buzzing flies? No? Great!*

*I have something to say before we begin. If you enjoy
these Charlie stories then I have a treat for you: a free
Charlie mini-book. My Dad would call it a corker: that
means it's excellent, and not just because I wrote it.
How do you get hold of one? You'll just have to read
the stories and find out! Here we go!*

Harry

Stuff you need to know

Hello. My name is Harry. I'm eight years old but I'll be nine in only ten months. I'm quite clever and quite normal. I can tell the time. I can tie my shoe laces. I don't have two heads or anything. My hair is long and wavy, although it sometimes gets tangly. My Dad says it's like straw in the morning and honey in the evening which is half-rude and half-nice. Typical Dad.

When the sun shines I get freckles on my nose. When I was little I didn't like them. I stood on the chair in the bathroom to look in the mirror. I rubbed them really hard with a flannel until my face was red and sore. I thought I'd got rid of them for a while, but then my face stopped being red and they came back. Mum came in and found me crying.

1

'What's the matter, Harry?' she asked.

'I've got spots,' I sobbed, and pointed to my nose. My cousin Freya complains about her spots whenever she comes for a sleepover although I can never see them.

Mum smiled which I didn't think was very nice because I was upset. But then  she gave me a cuddle, which felt better. 'They're not spots, they're summer sprinkles,' she said, 'and they make you look gorgeous.'

And then I started to think about sprinkles: sprinkles on cakes, sprinkles on fairies, and the water sprinkler in the garden. And I decided that having sprinkles on your face is a good thing.

I've just had a thought. You do know I'm a GIRL, don't you? People are always getting it wrong and it makes me quite cross. In fact my uncle Mike calls me 'Prince Harry' just to annoy me. He tells me to thump him really hard if I don't like it so I do, right in his tummy. But he just laughs until I jump on him and scream at him to stop.

My real name is actually Harriet, but everyone calls me Harry. Mum says that I could call myself Hattie if I wanted. But I think that sounds silly so I don't.

Actually not everyone calls me Harry; Granny always calls me Harriet. Whenever anyone talks about my name she shakes her head so that her curly white hair wobbles and she makes a funny sucking noise. There's a crazy story I want to tell you about Granny but Mum has just reminded me that this book is supposed to be about Charlie, my little brother. So let me tell you about him straight away.

Maybe you have a little brother. Mum says you might, but I bet he's not like Charlie. I'll explain.

Do you have a board at school where they put WOW words? You know, the interesting words that the teachers say you should use in your stories instead of *nice*? We do. It's like Charlie has rubbed himself all over with a glue stick and then rolled along that board because lots of them are perfect to describe him. Words like these:

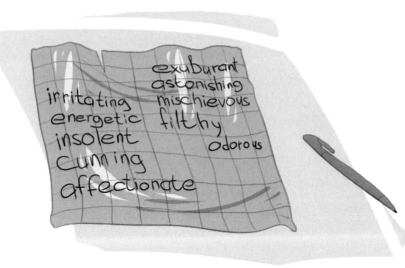

But there is another way to describe him, and you know it already because it's what I've decided to call this book: *Cheeky Charlie*. That's what Dad calls Charlie all the time: when he's shouted something rude, when he's done something naughty, when he wants him to budge up on the sofa, or just when he's ruffling Charlie's hair.

He tried that once with me and I went crazy. 'Alright Hattie, keep your hair on,' he said, and that made Mum laugh really loud which made me even angrier. So I stomped upstairs and played on his iPad without telling him, just to teach him a lesson.

But Charlie really is very cheeky, and that's what my book is about: all the naughty things that he has done. My teachers say that it's not nice to tell tales, but you don't know Charlie, so you can't get him into trouble.

But if you ever meet my Mum, don't tell her I've been a secret blabber-mouth, because then *I'll* get into trouble. Do you promise? Proper promise? Pinky promise?

Brilliant, because I've got loads to tell you. Some of it happened ages ago, some of it happened just last week. Some of it is funny, or sad, or even disgusting, because that's what Charlie can be. It might even make you a little bit sick, so get ready.

I once asked Dad to tell me about the naughtiest thing he had ever done.

'Me?' he said. 'I was an angel. I worked hard, did my homework on time, tidied my bedroom, went to bed early, got up late. Not like your mother. She was a right tearaway.'

I looked at Mum who was sitting on the sofa, making her eyes roll around in her head and pulling a funny face.

'Don't believe him, Harry,' said Mum. 'Here's what I know about your Dad. He ate his brother's birthday cake. He was sick on the dog. He almost crashed your Grandad's car. He was a right handful.'

'Handful of what?' I asked.

'Trouble,' said Mum.

Next door, where Charlie was watching telly, there was a crash.

'Charlie? Are you OK?' shouted Mum, getting up off the sofa.

'Yes Mummy!' shouted Charlie. 'I just falldid off the table.'

'Fell, Charlie, not falldid,' shouted Mum back. She sat back down. 'Now you know where Charlie gets it from.'

'Are you talking about my little Charlie?' said Dad. 'He's a goodie two-shoes like me. Although I wouldn't let him drive my car. Or let him near a dog. Or my birthday cake, come to think of it.'

'I think you're safe there, Dad,' I said. 'He'd be scared away by all the candles.'

'Oi!' said Dad, and he threw a cushion at me. It bounced off my arm onto the table and nearly knocked Mum's mug of tea over, the one with *Top*

Teacher written on it.

Mum looked at Dad and raised her eyebrows, making her forehead all wrinkly.

'Harry's arm was in the wrong place,' grumbled Dad. 'It wasn't my fault.'

Look, I haven't got long today, because I'm going for a haircut soon and I always get sweets so I don't want to miss it. But come back and I'll tell you lots of stories about what Charlie has done. And they're a lot, lot worse than you think.

Tattoo

I told this story at school last term in front of the whole class. Mrs Schofield asked if anyone 'had been up to anything interesting' during the holidays.

After I'd finished Mrs Schofield said, 'You told that well, Harry, but it was supposed to be a true story.'

'But it was a true story!' I protested. 'I can show you the photo… ' But wait a minute. I almost told you the ending and spoiled it.

So let's go back to the beginning. Mum and Dad decided that their bedroom was too small and that they didn't want to share a bathroom with us any more because children wee on toilet seats. You can't argue with that. Have you ever looked at the toilet seats at school? Yuck.

So Mum and Dad asked Jim from down the road to help. Jim is a builder. He has crazy curly ginger hair and a very big belly. He wears really old, tight t-shirts that have started to go see-through. Sometimes you can see his belly button through them and it looks like someone's pushed their finger into a balloon.

He drives an ancient white van and that has see-through bits and funny stains on it, too. In

the seat next to him there are two other men who work with him, but they're never the same. Maybe they don't like his t-shirts.

So Jim came round to look at our house. He stood outside, pointing at windows and walls, scribbling on a dirty piece of paper, and then he went away again. I forgot all about him until one sunny morning when he walked past the kitchen window while I was eating my breakfast.

'Mum, Jim is in our garden!' I shouted.

'What?' she said, and went outside. She soon came back in, shaking her head.

'What does he want?' I asked.

'He's starting the building work today,' Mum said. 'We just weren't expecting him, that's all.'

And that's how it began. Jim brought spades and pick axes and toolboxes and even an orange cement mixer down the side passage, helped by two men. One wore a blue tracksuit and the other wore a red tracksuit. Red Tracksuit stared right at me as he walked past. I ducked out of sight behind the washing machine.

When I felt brave enough to take another look I got an even bigger shock. Red and Blue had both taken their tops off and were now digging up the patio. Charlie came in and pressed his nose against the back door.

'Who dat?' he asked, pointing at Red. 'What he doing? Why someone done a dooring on him?' he continued.

Charlie asks a lot of questions and he doesn't always get the words right. But sure enough, Red did have a 'dooring' on his back: a tattoo of a lady. A lady with no clothes on.

Mum took Charlie out to meet the men. I stayed inside and watched as Charlie pointed at Red's tattoo. Everybody laughed and Jim picked Charlie up so he could touch it. He traced the outline of the lady with his finger while Red pretended that he was being tickled. Everyone laughed again, except me.

Over the next few days the holes in the garden got bigger and the piles of earth and clay grew higher. Eventually you could only see Red and Blue's sweaty faces as they worked – Jim never seemed to be around. They put planks of wood across the trenches so that we could get to the trampoline and the garden shed. Every day, whenever Red and Blue stopped for a cup of tea, Charlie would go up behind Red and run his finger over his tattoo. Red soon stopped pretending to laugh though.

I was in the kitchen, helping Mum make pizzas. It was *sweltering* – that's another pick from our WOW words – and Red and Blue were digging again in the sun. Charlie pulled Mum's apron.

'Hungry, Mummy! Me hungry Mummy!' he said.

'You could have an apple,' she said.

'Don't want a napple,' said Charlie.

'Or an orange?'

'Don't want a norange,' said Charlie.

'Or a banana?'

'Don't want a nana,' said Charlie.

'Well there's nothing else for you to eat, especially when you're being so rude. Go out and play until lunch is ready.'

Charlie toddled off through the open back door and went straight up to Red and Blue. They were sitting with their legs dangling into a hole, eating their lunch in the sunshine.

'Why you digging?' we heard him say. 'Haf you found any treasure? Why have you stopped?

Are you tired? Daddy is always tired. What's in your sandwiches? They smell yucky,' we heard him burble.

Red turned away from Charlie and shook his head. Charlie wrinkled his nose, which he does when he doesn't get what he wants, and stomped off to his den behind the shed. Blue disappeared towards the van; Red stretched out on the grass.

'Serves Charlie right,' said Mum, watching through the window. We put the pizza toppings on. Ham first, then cheese, but never mushrooms. Do you like mushrooms? I don't, they're weird. Who wants to eat grey food?

Charlie reappeared.

'Mummy, where my felt tips?'

'In the living room,' said Mum. 'Harry, keep on eye on him, will you?'

I wondered why he wanted felt tips. Mum didn't normally allow Charlie to use them on his own because once he drew smiley faces on the wall up the stairs. He sat on each step and got lots of practice because by the top they were really quite good. Dad went loopy crazy. 'But I did eyebrows and rainbow colours!' Charlie had said – though for once it didn't get him out of trouble.

Anyway, Charlie trotted back into the garden with the felt tips, crossed the plank, sat down next to the sleeping Red and pulled out a green pen.

Normally, when Charlie is naughty, I never see it happen. I don't know why. He's like a secret little spy who does stuff when you're not looking. But this time I saw everything. And because Red was grumpy, I didn't tell anyone. I just let him do it.

A little while later, Charlie and I were playing when we heard someone laughing hard and another man shouting. I couldn't understand the shouter, but he didn't sound happy. Charlie gave me a look – a little bit pleased, a little bit frightened.

Mum came downstairs to see what was happening and we went outside. Blue was crouching on the grass. At first I thought he was hurt because tears were streaming down his cheeks. But then I realised that he was the one who was laughing loudly. Red was doing that twisty-turny thing where you try to look at your own back, shouting at the top of his voice in another language.

'Do you know what's going on, Harry?' said Mum.

'It wasn't me,' I said. 'I didn't do anything.'

'Hmm,' said Mum, 'that's not what I asked. Charlie, any ideas?'

'Nuffink,' he said from behind Mum's leg. 'I done nuffink.'

He didn't look like he'd done nuffink though. He looked like he'd done somefink – and I knew what it was.

Red swivelled round. The naked lady on his back... well she wasn't naked any more. She wore a pair of bright green trousers and a purple and brown stripy top. And an orange hat. And she was carrying a blue handbag.

Charlie had also given her some big goggly eyes, a small beard, and big ears like an elephant.

'Why is the sun black? Couldn't you find your yellow felt tip?' asked Mum, and we looked up to see her rubbing her eyes. 'Oh dear, Charlie, what have you done this time?' she said, laughing.

Now I think you'd agree that drawing on somebody is pretty naughty. I was sure that Charlie was in the biggest trouble of his life. But something strange happened.

When Dad got home, Mum showed him a photo of Red's back. And instead of going mad Dad roared with laughter, just like Blue had. He

couldn't stop. He grabbed Charlie. 'Come here my little doodle bug!' he shouted and they fell onto the sofa, laughing like crazy.

'That's your best yet,' said Dad between chuckles. 'You made her look like the elephant man.'

'She not a man she a lady!' protested Charlie. 'And I did a big smile on her!'

'I know you did,' said Dad, holding Charlie upside down and swinging him from side to side, 'and you didn't colour over the lines. You're a proper little artist, Cheeky Charlie!'

Treasure

Not long after the tattoo incident, Charlie was in trouble again. Big trouble. And this time Dad wasn't laughing one little bit.

You need to know that Charlie had become obsessed with pirates. He had books about pirates, DVDs about pirates, even a scratchy pirate costume with an eye patch that he wore to preschool.

He even talked like a pirate. 'More cornflakes, pea hearties!' he'd shout at breakfast.

'Yo ho ho and a bottle of yum!' he'd yell at lunch.

'I'm burying the treasure!' he'd declare at dinner when Mum caught him trying to push his peas under the baked potato skins.

The sun that had been shining when Charlie coloured Red's back had gone. Day after day the rain tipped down, filling the builders' holes with brown, muddy water.

To Charlie this was just another pirate adventure waiting to happen. As soon as the rain stopped and Mum opened the back door, Charlie rushed into the garden.

'I'm off to find the treasure!' he shouted, his slightly-too-big pirate hat sliding off his head. 'Come on Harry, let's find the treasure!'

'No thanks,' I said. 'It's wet, cold and muddy, and there's no treasure in our garden.'

But he wasn't listening. 'Pirate Charlie cross the bang plank!' I heard him shout. He wobbled his way across the trenches and rushed off up the garden, waving his toy spade.

I went inside to watch telly. A few minutes later I heard Mum in the kitchen.

'Charlie, just look at the state of you! What on earth have you been doing?'

Charlie mumbled something I couldn't hear.

'But that's not treasure, darling, it's an old flowerpot.'

I laughed. Brothers can be so stupid.

'And that's a bit of glass, you shouldn't even be playing with that... and that's – hang on, what is that?' said Mum. 'Let's give it a wash and see.'

That sounded more interesting. I walked through to the kitchen where Charlie was standing on the stool at the sink. His arms were crusted with brown mud; his shorts were wet right through and he had a big smear of mud on his face, too – probably because he'd been picking his nose.

'What's that, Mum?' I asked. 'Is it money?'

'It my treasure,' said Charlie, looking pleased.

Mum was holding a big brown coin, rubbing it and peering closely.

'Hey Charlie, you're right, it is treasure. It's an old penny!'

'What, one penny?' I said. 'Just 1p?'

'Yes, but it's nearly 80 years old,' replied Mum. 'Charlie, that's brilliant. Well done!'

'Wow Charlie that's amaaazing,' I said. 'You've found 1p, you're so clever. I've got 80p in my piggy bank.'

'If you can't say anything nice, Harry, then don't bother,' said Mum.

I went back to the telly.

That evening, Dad made a massive fuss of my brother, telling him he was a tip-top pirate and an expert treasure finder. They rolled around on the carpet shouting, 'Ha haaaar!' and being idiots.

I couldn't stand it.

'Shush!' I shouted. 'I can't hear the telly!'

'Oooh,' said Dad, 'one of the crew is revolting! Shall we throw her overboard?'

He tried to grab me but I was too quick and ran out of the room. He can be so annoying!

The next day, Charlie rushed out into the garden after breakfast. The builders still weren't back so he had the whole muddy place to himself. Very soon his pirate outfit was ruined, his hat had fallen into a puddle and he'd lost his eyepatch. He won't be wearing that again for World Book Day.

But the hunt went on and he poked around with his spade in every nook and cranny, muttering 'Pea hearties' to himself.

More than once, he ran in excitedly to show Mum his loot.

'That's a bottle top,' said Mum the first time.

'That's an old piece of string,' said Mum. 'Not sure we'll get much for that.'

'That's... ugh, Charlie, what is that? It stinks!' she said, taking the next dirty object out of Charlie's grip. 'Oh Charlie, that's an old chicken bone or something. It was probably left by a fox.'

'Not a chicken bone, is a dinosaur,' said Charlie. 'From a pirate dinosaur. Rrrarrgh.'

'That disgusting thing is not staying in this house a moment longer,' said Mum. I thought she meant Charlie for a moment. 'It's time to come in and get yourself cleaned up.'

That afternoon I played in my room while Charlie stomped around the house. Sometimes I'd hear Mum shout for him and every time he'd be in a different room. I ignored him, especially when he wanted someone to wipe his bottom. Yuck.

After Dad got home, Charlie sneaked back into the garden again. He was back suspiciously quickly.

'I finded more treasure!' he declared.

'What've you got there, little fella?' said Dad.

Charlie opened up his grubby fist to reveal a not-very-dirty medal, still with the ribbon attached. I recognised it straight away.

'That's Grandad's!' I said. 'You're not supposed to touch those, is he Dad?' I said.

Mum, who was watching, disappeared into the hall without a word.

'Have you been rummaging in our bedroom, Charlie?'

Charlie stood there, his head hanging down, saying nothing.

'Charlie? This is serious. Tell Daddy what you've been up to.'

I don't know why Dad was asking. Charlie had taken Grandad's medal and pretended to find it. It actually belonged to Dad's Grandad, who got it when he won an aeroplane fight in a war. He's dead now which is why we have it, along with two other medals he won in other fights. He was a good fighter, my Dad says, which is a bit weird because fighters get sent to the headteacher at my school.

Mum was standing at the door, holding Grandad's blue medal case. She opened it up and showed it to Dad. Empty.

'OK Charlie, let's go. You need to show me where the medals are.'

'Can I look?' I asked.

'No, you stay here,' said Dad. 'I'm sure we'll be back in five minutes, won't we Charlie?'

Charlie didn't look sure at all but they put on their wellies and went out into the garden. By now it was almost dark. I watched them walk up and down with Dad pointing at holes and piles of mud and Charlie plodding along, looking down.

They weren't back in five minutes, or ten, or fifteen.

'No joy,' said Dad when they reappeared. 'Guess what I'm doing tomorrow.'

Next morning, Dad was out in the garden with a spade, searching. At first, Charlie was with him, poking at the soil with a garden cane. I watched from the doorway.

'Maybe I putted it here,' he said. 'Or here. Or here. Or… '

'That's enough, Charlie,' said Dad. 'Time to go in, please.'

'But I…'

'No. Inside. Now.'

When Dad uses that voice even Charlie knows it's serious.

Dad hadn't been out there very long when we heard him shout. 'Bingo!'

Through the window we saw him grinning, holding up a medal. 'One more to find!'

But the last one didn't want to be found. He was out there while we went swimming. He was out there until Mum called him in for lunch. And he went out again afterwards.

I found him later at the table, drinking tea.

'What you been doing Daddy?' said Charlie.

'Looking for Grandad's medal, silly,' I said. 'Did you find it, Dad?'

'Nope,' he said. 'Not a sniff.'

Charlie sniffed, loudly, and started to laugh. But it didn't last long because Mum gave him one of her strict looks.

'I wonder if there's another way,' said Mum.

'How's that then?' said Dad. 'Get a digger in?'

'Not exactly,' said Mum. 'Didn't Alan say he used to go metal detecting?'

Slowly, Dad put down his tea. 'You're right,' he said. 'You're a genius. I'll call him now.'

Alan is one of our neighbours. He lives with his wife, Sheila, and they are always in their front garden when I walk to school, planting flowers or mowing the lawn.

Alan came round and brought his metal detector. Have you seen one? They look like a plate on the end of a stick. You put these headphones on and wave the stick around and it helps you to find stuff underground.

'Thanks for coming, Alan,' said Dad. 'I couldn't live with myself if we lost his Aircrew medal.'

'Aye, that's a good'un,' said Alan.

Once, when I was walking past Alan and Sheila's house, I asked Mum why Alan says 'I' instead of 'yes'. But I must have said it too loud because Alan smiled, put down his trowel, and told me that's how they talk where he comes from, in 'God's own country'.

'God's country? What, heaven?' I asked. 'Have

you been dead?'

'I come from Yorkshire and it is a lot like heaven, only it's a bit handier for the motorway.'

I had no idea what he was talking about.

'I'm from up north,' he said. 'Where the people say *gr-ass* instead of *gr-arse*.'

Now then. Mary rode on an ass in the Bible, I know that because they told us at school. An ass is a type of donkey, but arse is a rude word for bottom. Why was Alan talking about donkeys and grass and bottoms? I gave up trying to understand.

Very soon Alan was out in our garden with his headphones on. I wondered if he was listening to Taylor Swift. She's my favourite.

Just like Dad, he was out there for ages. Charlie and I sat on the step watching him. Just as I was getting bored he bent down, dug about a bit with a spade and picked something up.

It didn't look like a medal. It looked like a bit of old shoe.

'It's probably from a fox,' I shouted. 'We have loads of them.'

'Not this one, lassie,' said Alan. 'Give your Dad a shout, will you?'

I fetched Dad while Alan kicked off his muddy

wellies and came into the kitchen.

'Have you found it, fella?' asked Dad.

'Can't say that I have,' said Alan, 'but it's still worth a gander.'

Here we go again. A gander is a boy goose. Mrs Schofield told us that. But if this dirty thing was worth a gander, like Alan said, how much is that? One pound? Twenty pounds? I've never tried to buy a goose, have you?

Dad and Mum gathered around while Charlie and I stood on chairs for a better look.

The dirty object he'd found was a bag. Alan used his thumbs to push bits of soil off it and unpicked a piece of cord that tied it closed.

He tipped the bag and a handful of coins slid out onto the table.

'TREASURE!' shouted Charlie.

'Easy there flower,' said Alan. 'Let's see what we've got.'

'Penny…1914,' he said, peering at the first coin. 'Another penny…1922. They're all pennies,' he said.

I counted quickly. One, two, three… 'Nine pennies!' I said. 'That's not even enough for a finger of fudge!'

'Steady on now,' said Alan. 'Some of these are worth a few quid, I reckon. We've got some here from Queen Victoria and a couple older than that. You should get them valued, Tom. You might be a happy man.'

'Well well,' said Dad. 'I can't say I'm happy about losing the medal but this is a bit of a result, isn't it, gang?'

Later, after Alan had left carrying his metal detector and a pack of beer that Dad had given him to say thanks, we all looked at the coins again and Dad gave them a wipe with a cloth.

'Where are we going to keep them?' asked Mum. 'That leather bag is falling apart. We need to put them somewhere out of harm's way.' She looked hard at Charlie.

'Stick 'em in the medal case for now,' said Dad. 'They'll fit where that missing one should go.'

Mum opened the medal case. She frowned and looked a little more closely. I leaned over. There, sticking out between the case and the shiny blue medal holder inside, was a small piece of black, blue and yellow ribbon.

Mum used her fingernail to hook it out from behind the holder. Attached to the ribbon was Grandad's missing star medal. Mum swung it gently from her finger until Dad noticed.

'You have got to be kidding me,' he said. He walked up behind Charlie, and put his arms around him.

'Looks like the booty was right under our noses all along. And we found a little bit more along the way, didn't we Charlie? Maybe I won't throw you to the sharks just yet, my little pirate friend.'

Flying

Last summer, we went on an aeroplane. I'd been on an aeroplane loads of times before of course, but for Charlie this was eye-poppingly exciting. 'Airlane Airlane!' he kept shouting at breakfast until Mum told him to *shhh!* and eat his Cheerios.

All the way to the airport Charlie wriggled and shuffled and shouted and moaned until even Dad said that if Charlie didn't shut up, we'd turn round and go home again. I knew he didn't mean it – he says that all the time – and maybe Charlie knew it too because he started blowing raspberries. We all ignored him and I looked out of the window.

The airport was busier than a supermarket after school. There were grown-ups everywhere but none of them looked happy about going on holiday. Children were running around, riding on

suitcases and lying on trollies. Mum held on to the
back of our jumpers and pulled us close.

We joined the back of a big queue that wriggled
like a lumpy, grumpy snake towards desk number
68. In front of us were a big woman and a skinny
man. The big woman was sitting on a little wheelie
suitcase, her bottom curving down on both sides
until it was nearly touching the floor. The case was
squished and the zip was coming undone with a

piece of red cloth was sticking out.

It reminded me of Magic Melvyn, the magician at my last birthday party. He had pulled a red hanky out of Charlie's ear, but Charlie doesn't like surprises so he thumped him. Magic went really red then, just like his hanky, and Dad shouted so loud that some of my friends started crying, too.

But I was telling you about our trip on the aeroplane. In front of us, the skinny man took some money from the woman and walked off towards the shops.

Charlie couldn't stop staring. 'Mummy,' he said, pointing. 'Mummy. Mummy. Mummy!'

'For goodness sake. What is it, Charlie?'

'Dat suitcase is going, "Ow, ow, is hurty, peas don't sit on me!"'

The woman didn't turn round but she moved her head a bit and I could tell she was listening.

'Shh!' said Mum. 'That's a very rude thing to say about *me*, Charlie. We don't say things like that, it's not kind or polite.'

'Mum,' I said, 'he didn't mean you, he meant –'

'No he definitely meant me, Harry,' said Mum.

She turned to Charlie. 'Just wait nicely and you

can have some crisps on the plane.'

'Cripps! Cripps! Cripps!' said Charlie, and he plonked his bottom on the floor. I told you he was a rude boy.

I tried to ignore him. I was just trying to get the wheels to all go in a straight line on our trolley when I heard a very loud, very angry voice.

'Look what your kid has done!'

I looked up. The big lady was standing up now with her hands on her hips. Her face was all crumpled and on her huge, purple bottom lip you could see a disgusting bubble of spit.

I looked down at Charlie and at first I thought he was sitting on a rug. Except that this one appeared to be made of knickers. Red pants, blue pants, black pants, stripy pants. Charlie had chosen a pair with spots on like a leopard and was stretching them over his head. Although he didn't need to stretch them much because they were enormous, like a big spotty tent. You could just see his grinning face through a leg hole.

'Charlie!' scolded Mum. 'Put those back!'

The big woman snatched her pants back and started to stuff them all through the broken zip.

'I'm so sorry,' said my Mum, 'I think he was

just being curious. Charlie, say sorry to the lady.'

'Sorry lady,' said naughty Charlie, not sounding at all sorry.

'People like you need to keep your children under control,' said the woman.

'Now hang on a second,' said Mum, 'he was only –'

But Dad put his hand on her arm and in a flash he stepped in front of Mum and scooped Charlie up into his arms.

'He's very sorry and we are too. Aren't we, Cheeky Charlie?' He smiled his Big Daddy smile and ruffled Charlie's hair.

Later on, as we walked across the tarmac towards the plane, we found ourselves behind the funny couple again. They headed for the front staircase; Mum steered us all towards the back.

On board, the seats were nearly full. 'It cost us fifteen quid to get on first,' grumbled Dad as we waited for people to sit down. 'Fat lot of good that turned out to be.'

'I explained as fast as I could,' replied Mum in the voice she uses when she's going to get really cross. 'If someone had been watching Charlie properly this morning, he wouldn't have put all those knives and forks into my handbag, would he? And then Mummy wouldn't have had to answer all those questions when the security alarm went off.' She pulled me to one side.

'Come on Harry, let's sit here.'

We sat down with Dad and Charlie finding a place several rows further forward. Mum gave me a sweet from her handbag.

'Shall I give one to the boys?' she asked me. I shook my head.

'No, I agree. These sweets are only for girls.'

The flight was very long and very boring. Later, after they'd given us our lunch, Mum nudged me. 'Look at that,' she said smiling. One of the pretty waitresses was talking to Charlie. Dad was looking at the waitress, grinning.

Just then she got up to let someone past – it was the big lady. Inside the aeroplane, she looked bigger than ever: her legs bish-bashed people's elbows and bumped shoulders. She was grabbing the top of each seat as if she was climbing a ladder.

She pushed her way past the waitress who nearly fell into Dad's lap but she didn't say sorry. 'What a vile woman,' I heard Mum mutter.

Charlie pulled on Dad's sleeve. He mouthed the word 'toilets' to us; Mum pointed towards the front of the plane and off they went.

Dad told us later what happened next. There was a queue for the toilet so while Dad chatted to another waitress Charlie had gone exploring and found the skinny man fast asleep with his mouth open, like he was at the dentist. The seat next to him was empty, but on the tray in front of it was the big woman's dinner, all ready to eat.

I bet you can guess what happened. You're right: Charlie plonked himself down and started eating. First he ate the chocolate pudding – but he was still hungry. Then he ate the biscuits – but he was still hungry. He even ate the carrots. Then he pushed all the mashed potato onto the tray with his fingers and tried to make a 'well' for the gravy, like Mum does for the egg when she's making a cake. But he must have left a gap because the gravy ran out when he poured it on top. Only the tray stopped it dribbling all over the seat.

I'll tell you one thing Charlie didn't eat: the lump of cheese. He doesn't like cheese but he thought the skinny man would. Or perhaps he thought it would give him funny dreams, like Mum says. Whatever he was thinking, Charlie plonked this big lump of smelly yellow cheese straight into the skinny man's mouth.

Has anyone ever dropped cheese into your mouth when you are asleep? Me neither, but I bet it's not nice. The skinny man didn't like it because he woke up, coughing and spluttering.

Other passengers around started to say 'There,

there,' and offered him water. But then he started saying some very rude words so they said 'OK mate, calm down,' and 'I've got children here, do you mind?' and they went back to their dinners.

That's when Dad noticed Charlie, smeared with chocolate and mashed potato. Dad did that scoopy-uppy thing again with Charlie, and just in time because the big woman had just returned to her seat. Can you guess how happy she was to find that her dinner was gone?

Mum said later that the woman was 'apoplectic'.

'Can I have a popple lectic?' asked Charlie.

'What does it mean, Dad?' I asked.

'It means you are very, very angry,' said Dad.

'Very very very very very very angry,' repeated Charlie. 'Very very very very – '

'That's enough, Charlie,' said Dad, ruffling his hair. 'You've got us into quite enough trouble already today, Your Cheekiness.'

Charlie wasn't listening. How do I know? Because he did one more very naughty thing I'll tell you about before I go and have my tea.

It happened when we were waiting for our bags. Dad said he was desperate for a wee so Mum, Charlie and I waited by the conveyor belt. Have you ever seen one? They're really cool; they go round and round with the luggage and if you're lucky some of the bags fall off at the corners.

This conveyor belt came out through a hole in the wall, went around a big loop, and then disappeared again. The holes were covered in long flaps, a bit like the doors at the back of supermarkets where you're not supposed to go.

I'll tell you about Charlie getting lost in the supermarket another time, but the important bit of that story is that they found him on the other side of the flaps, trying to open a packet of Wotsits.

Maybe he thought he'd find some more Wotsits in the airport? I looked up to see him lying on his tummy on a big blue suitcase, with his arms and legs stretched out like Superman. He disappeared through the flaps head first with his feet kicking a little bit as if he wanted to go faster.

'Mum! Look at Charlie!' And I pointed.

'What?' said Mum, who was reading her book.

'He went through the hole on a bag!' I explained. Mum told me not to move an inch and she started running towards the end of the belt.

Before she could get there, the flaps started to lift up to reveal a big black case... and on it sat Charlie! He was cross-legged, just like you have to do in assembly, and looked very pleased with himself. You must admit it was a clever trick to swap cases so quickly.

But as we watched, a big pair of hairy arms came through the flaps and pulled him back! I screamed. I heard Mum scream too, and she started climbing onto the conveyor belt.

'Mummy watch out, he'll get you too!' I yelled.

But Mum didn't go through the flaps. Instead she climbed right over the belt and was now in the middle of the loop, clambering over all the adverts.

She had one leg on each side of a woman holding a plate of salad when a door next to the belt opened. Through it came a giant man in blue overalls, carrying a grinning Charlie in his arms. The man pressed the big red button on the wall. The conveyor belt made a groaning noise and stopped.

Mum must have been quite tired from her climbing because she was really red and sweaty by the time she got back to me, just as Dad got back from the toilet.

'What's the matter with you?' asked Dad.

'Don't even go there,' said Mum.

I pointed at the hole in the wall to help Dad.

'Just don't even go there.'

'Charlie been playing up again, has he?' said Dad. Hair ruffle. 'What a Cheeky Charlie you are.'

Water Slide

Have you ever stayed in a hotel? We have. It was last year, in the summer. We flew to Spain in an aeroplane. It was night when we arrived. As we stood at the top of the steps waiting to get off you could feel the warm wind on your face; there was a funny smell, too. 'Just like one of Mummy's trumps, but nicer,' said Dad.

But forget about that, because I want to tell you about the amazing hotel. There was a machine where you could buy crisps and drinks whenever you wanted and a restaurant where you could have cherry yoghurt and ham for breakfast – *every morning*. And if you wanted toast you had to do it yourself, which was fine with me because I'm an expert chef.

We only used the toaster for a few days, though,

because halfway through our holiday there was a big sign on it saying *No funciona*, which means 'Not working' in Spanish. Lots of springs and metal bits were hanging out and next to it, on the tray, were all sorts of blackened, twisted things that had been put through the toaster.

Charlie and I poked around: we could see a plastic spoon, a piece of someone's sunglasses, one of those special cards that you use to get into hotel bedrooms instead of keys, and...

'Is my hellyfant!' said Charlie, picking up a lump of stinky grey plastic.

Now most children would be very grumpy if their favourite toy was ruined – even if it was their fault, because they had been trying to make elephant on toast. Not Charlie.

'Look, my hellyfant is all melty!' he shouted, and he ran back to Mum with a grin on his face.

I saw her look at the lump. She looked at the toaster. And then she shook her head. Charlie put his melty hellyfant into the change bag.

But the best thing about our hotel wasn't the toaster, it was the swimming pool. I don't know what the swimming pool in your town is like, but the one near my house is boring. It's a rectangle with ropes in it. Grown-ups swim from end to end looking like they need a poo. You can't run, you can't jump, you can't splash. Bor-ring.

But not the one at this hotel. It was shaped like a jelly that has been dropped on the floor, with curvy edges and extra little blobby pools around the outside that Mum called Jacuzzis but Charlie called 'bubble baths'. All around, raised up on stilts, were two twisty, turny water slides: a blue one called The Hamster, and a green one called The Dragon.

The Hamster was long and slow. People waved at their friends as they travelled on the special mats. At the end you plopped out into one of the big pools next to the stairs, ready to have another go.

But The Dragon was very different. Even at the start, the place where you put your mat, it was really steep and fierce jets of water squirted out right next to your bottom.

On the first day we sat in the chairs by the pool and you could see people holding on to the bars at the top and trying to sit on their mats. But the water made them slip, and they usually disappeared into the tube sideways or backwards, screaming. Then you heard them scream some more as they went around the bends. At the bottom they shot out of a dragon's mouth into the main pool, right in front of everyone, still screaming. They made a massive 'kersploosh!' as they landed, and went right under the water. That usually stopped them screaming.

Even though I'm really good at swimming, I didn't want to go on The Dragon. I was a bit afraid of The Hamster too, which is strange because I'm not afraid of real hamsters, even when they do a wee on my school uniform like my friend's hamster does.

'It's just like the slides at the soft play, but with water,' said my Dad as we all sat in one of the Jacuzzis. He does talk rubbish sometimes.

Charlie was trying to press the button to turn on the bubbles. He only has chubby little fingers so I pressed it for him.

'No I wanna do it!' he screamed in my face.

I stuck my tongue out at him and he screamed again. He's really easy to annoy sometimes. Mum was just telling him to calm down when the bubbles started. They came out everywhere: by your feet, on your back, even up your bum a bit when you sat in the special seats. The water turned completely white with bubbles so you couldn't even see your knees.

'Check me out!' said Dad, floating on his back. Dad was wearing massive blue shorts with pink flowers on them – his 'baggies', he called them.

Something odd was happening. Dad's baggies were getting bigger. Much, much bigger. They were blowing up like James' Giant Peach, or a hot air balloon.

'Did you have beans for breakfast?' asked Mum.

'Beans, beans, good for your heart, the more you eat –' I shouted. My friend Jade taught me that. You couldn't hear the last words because Mum put her hand over my mouth.

By now Dad's shorts were so big it looked like he was going to explode. He poked them and they puffed straight back up again.

Do you ever do pile-ons with grown-ups? It's where you all shout 'Pile on!' and climb on top. If you're at the bottom you can hardly breathe and you have to scream until they get off.

Charlie loves a pile-on and from where he stood on the side this looked like the perfect chance. 'Pie Ron!', he yelled, throwing himself right onto

Dad's inflatable shorts.

'Ooof!' shouted Dad as the weight of Charlie bent him in half.

'Cool!' I shouted.

'Oh Charlie,' sighed Mum.

Charlie probably shouted something else too but we didn't hear him because he had disappeared under the bubbles.

Dad reached under the water, scooped him out and sat him on his lap. Water was running down his face, which Charlie hates.

'That was a bit daft wasn't it, Charlie?' said Dad, giving him a cuddle.

Charlie sniffed a bit, then went quiet.

'I done a wee,' he said quietly.

'I think it's time for us to get out now,' said Mum firmly.

After we'd had a toasted sandwich in the café we went back out to the main pool. There were sun loungers lined up in a row. We threw our towels over the ones at the end and climbed on.

'What are we going to do?' I asked.

'Well I don't know about you but I'm going to catch some rays and have a kip,' said Dad, leaning back and closing his eyes.

'You can go and play,' said Mum, 'but make sure you stay where I can see you.' And she picked up her magazine.

We were by the pool where The Dragon ended but nobody was coming down the slide. Grown-ups were just sitting around; some of them were reading, but many of them were asleep. It was hot and there was nothing to do.

I picked up Dad's mirror sunglasses and tried them on. They made everything look dark like night was coming and it was nearly time for bed. Why would you want that?

'Do I look cool?' I asked Mum. She just smiled and carried on reading.

Charlie copied me. He's always copying me. Do you have a little brother or sister that does that? It drives me mad. He pulled Mum's sunglasses off her face and put them on. They were way too big and kept falling off his nose.

'If you break those I'm going to be hopping mad,' said Mum. That was a mistake, of course, because then Charlie started trying to hop round and he screwed up his nose to make himself look mad. The sunglasses fell onto the floor.

'Shoo!' said Mum, examining them for scratches. 'Go and make mischief somewhere else, I'm off duty.'

'That's a bit rude,' I said. 'Come on Charlie, let's explore.'

I grabbed his hand and we walked along the edge of the pool.

Now here's something else that's really annoying about Charlie: everyone likes him. People smile, pat his wavy, hairy head, or tell Mum what a 'cutie' they think he is. Charlie doesn't even say thank you! He just stands there looking really serious, like he does when he's trying to decide which flavour milkshake he wants.

This time was no different.

'Hello!' said the old lady on the blue towel.

'Hola!' said the woman on the red towel. (Hola means 'Hello' in Spain, my Mum told me that.)

A man with the headphones winked at him and made a *chick-chick* sound out of the side of his mouth.

Charlie just kept on walking.

The last sunlounger was empty. I sat down but

Charlie crawled underneath and started to tickle my legs.

'Charlie! Stop it!' I said. 'You're not at home now! Get out!'

At home Charlie is always crawling under the table. He'll sit there pretending to be a dog and licking your knee or chewing the laces on your shoes. Once, when Mum had lots of friends for tea, he started to shout out what colour pants Mum's friends were wearing. 'Blue pants! Black pants! Black pants again!' he'd said, and all Mum's friends had started screaming with laughter.

'Little pants! Big pants!' he'd continued, but then he started getting silly, like he always does. 'Stinky pants! Poo poo pants! She got no pants on!'

At that point Mum had pulled him out from under the table and asked him to say sorry to her friends with the stinky pants and the poo poo pants. The woman with no pants on said that he had made a mistake, and that they were just too small for Charlie to see.

So it wasn't a surprise when Charlie climbed under my sun lounger. I found something to do because I realised you can dip your toe into the pool and then draw pictures on the tiles in water. They fade quite quickly, but you just get your toe wet and do it again.

I'm not sure how long I was painting pictures for, but I stopped when a man got out of the pool and walked his wet, hairy monster feet right over my painting. He ruined it. I looked up to see Charlie and realised that he'd crawled back to Mum and Dad through the tunnel of sun loungers.

As I walked back towards them the first woman I walked past was looking for something, muttering angrily to herself. The next woman put on a pair of sunglasses and the first woman started pointing at her face, and getting shouty.

On the next sun lounger, a man was sleep with a hat over his face. A large, bright pink hat with a floppy rim.

Next in the row was a woman reading a book.

I nearly tripped over her shoes and that was hardly surprising because they were huge blue Crocs. They looked like canoes. My Grandad has massive feet but these were extraordinary. It didn't make sense: this woman, asleep on her sun lounger, was tiny! Her little legs ended in little feet with little painted toes. It seemed a shame she couldn't get shoes the right size.

Next to her was the English couple who had sat near us at breakfast. She was doing that thing where women lie on their front and undo their tops. I don't know why they do that – perhaps the straps are a bit itchy. The man was putting suncream on her back. But just as he picked up the bottle the woman with the tiny feet reached out and snatched it out of his hand!

'Oi! What are you playing at?' he shouted.

Tiny toes shouted something back in Spanish that I didn't understand – but I don't think she was asking if he liked cherry yoghurt for breakfast.

'What's the matter, Gary?' asked the woman, twisting her neck round to see.

'This nutter has just stolen our suncream!' said Gary, pointing at tiny toes. 'Seriously, she just grabbed it!'

'But that's not our suncream, babe,' said the woman. 'Ours is in an orange bottle.'

'It must be,' said Gary. 'It was under my towel!'

Tiny toes was now standing besides the woman. She had her hands on her hips and a very red face. Perhaps she did need more suncream after all.

'You wan my suncream?' she said. 'Here, have my suncream,' and she took the top off the bottle and poured the white liquid out all over the woman's back. It went everywhere, splashing onto her towel and dripping onto the ground.

Have you ever dropped a vanilla ice cream? I have. Mum had to cut the bits off that might have touched dog wee and then she scooped the rest back into the cone with her fingers. It still tasted the same. Anyway, that's what this suncream looked like, splooshed all over the place.

'Aaargh! Are you out of your mind?' the woman cried, getting up. But then she remembered that she didn't have a top on so she snatched her towel, tipping all her stuff onto the ground.

'Watch out Soph, that's my phone!' said the man as his shiny mobile clattered onto the tiles.

'That's not your phone, Gary. Not unless you've bought a Minnie Mouse case. Why have you got someone else's phone?'

Something seriously strange was going on and it was happening to everyone I walked past. People all around the pool were talking and pointing at each other. I hurried past a man who was wearing big pink sunglasses and rubbing his eyes. I heard another tell his friend, 'But I put the car keys just there! If we can't find them, we're stuffed. We should call the police.'

Finally I reached Mum and Dad. I watched as people argued, swapped sunglasses, lifted up their sun loungers and emptied their bags.

'Why has everyone got ants in their pants?' asked Dad.

'I'm not sure,' said Mum, 'but… Charlie, does this have anything to do with you?'

Charlie was looking at the sky, picking his nose.

'Charlie? I'm talking to you. Have you been up to your shenanigans again?'

Slowly, Charlie put his finger in his mouth, sucked it, and smiled a big smile. 'I want nanny kittens!' he said. 'I love nanny kittens!'

'Nanny kittens?' said Dad. 'What have kittens got to do with the price of fish?'

'Don't like fishies,' said Charlie.

'Are we having fish tonight, Dad?' I asked.

Mum groaned loudly. 'Why can't you lot talk normally? Give me strength,' she said. So Charlie ran over and started to squeeze her muscles.

A bunch of people at the other end of the pool were pointing at us. 'Hmm... I think it's about time we did a runner,' said Dad, quickly gathering up our things. 'Come on kids, let's skedaddle.'

'Ski-what?' I said. 'What's a daddle, Dad?' Now *I* was confused. Was Dad talking Spanish?

'Never mind that now,' said Dad, pulling Charlie by the hand. 'Let's get out of here.'

A bunch of car keys fell out of Charlie's shorts.

'Ow!' he said as they landed on his toes.

Before we could say anything Dad gave them a little kick with the side of his foot and slid them under our neighbour's sun lounger.

'Come on kids, time to explore,' he announced, pulling us firmly by the hand away. 'Nothing here for us to worry about.'

'I'll tell you what,' said Dad as we walked past the tower, 'let's go on the slides.'

'Yay!' shouted Charlie. 'I want go on The Dragon!'

'I am *not* going on The Dragon,' I said firmly.

'Me neither,' said Mum. 'It looks horrific. And the kids are too small.'

'I'm not small I'm FREE!' shouted Charlie, stamping his foot.

'You may be three, but you're still not big enough. Maybe next year.'

'Ah relax,' said Dad. 'I'll go down with them. You can wait for us at the bottom.'

'Yay! Yay-yay-yay! Yay-de-yay-yay!' shouted Charlie.

Have you noticed how much Charlie shouts? I once told Charlie that his belly button was a volume control. I stuck my finger in it and twiddled it around to see if he'd be quiet. But then he started shouting at me. So I told him his button must be broken.

Mum put a swimming jacket on Charlie and helped me with my armbands and then took all our bags. We grabbed Dad's hand and set off up the steps.

'One two three four five seven ten eleventy twenty,' counted Charlie as we went up. He's rubbish at numbers.

'I reckon you could do The Dragon,' said Dad to me.

'But it looks really scary,' I said. 'I might get stuck in the tube.'

'It's not like *Charlie and the Chocolate Factory* you know, Harry. And you're a skinny minnie, anyway. Come on, it'll be fun, and I'll hold you the whole way down.'

'Only if you promise to lift me up at the end so I don't get water up my schnozz,' I said. 'Pinky promise.'

'Pinky promise,' said Dad.

And so we climbed past the entrance to The Hamster, all the way to the top of The Dragon.

We were seriously high. You could see right out of the hotel over the roofs of the town towards the sea. The metal platform had little gaps and you could see people climbing up the steps underneath you. In front of us, two more steps led up to The Dragon; there were handles to grab so you could sit down and get ready. I could just see the first bend and the entrance to the green tunnel.

I grabbed the railing and looked down to find

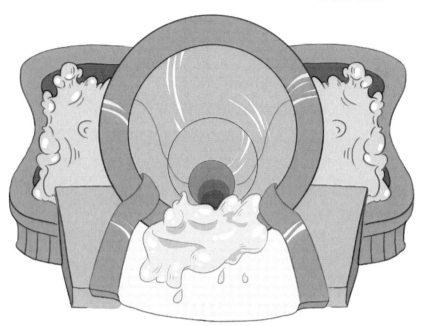

Mum. Big mistake. I got the 'humpy bridge' feeling in my tummy. Does yours do that? It feels like your insides are rolling over and over like socks in a washing machine.

I grabbed Dad's arm. 'I'm scared,' I said. Even Charlie was a bit quieter than normal. All you could hear were the jets of water and the far-away cries of children at the bottom.

'Ah, come on,' said Dad. 'It'll be brilliant. Now, how are we going to do this? Perhaps I should have thought this through a little bit more.' He picked up a mat from the pile.

'Right. I'll get onto the mat and hold onto the

bars. Charlie, you climb on and sit between my legs so you're at the front. Harry, you're on last. Climb over me into the middle and grab Charlie round the waist. Easy peasy.'

And before we could say anything he'd let go of our hands, climbed up the steps, and plonked himself down on his mat in the water jets at the top of the slide.

'Whoah, these babies are strong!' he said, grabbing onto the bars.

'What babies?' said Charlie.

'He means the jets,' I said. Dad's always talking about babies instead of the proper words. I don't know why.

'Right, Charlie boy, climb on board the Daddy train!'

Charlie clambered up the steps behind Dad and stood there, not quite knowing what to do.

'Just crawl over me,' said Dad. He grabbed the bar above his head with one hand and took Charlie's arm with the other. Charlie wriggled down Dad's body towards the space on the mat at the front, between Dad's knees. Everything was wet and slippery and Charlie's little hands were grabbing and prodding, trying to get a grip.

'Ooh!' said Dad as Charlie climbed on top.

'Fnurgh!' said Dad as Charlie's knee squashed Dad's nose.

'Aieee! Don't grab that!' said Dad when Charlie grabbed hold of the hairs on Dad's chest.

'Finally!' said Dad as Charlie twizzled around and sat himself down, grabbing Dad's shorts to stop him sliding off down the tube.

'Right Harry, you're up. Do the same as Charlie, but try not to break every bone in my body,' said Dad.

I was seriously scared but I didn't want to show it because there was now a big queue behind us. I took a big step over Dad's head, swung my other leg over and sat down on Dad's chest.

'Shuffle down!' said a voice from under my bottom. So I did a bum shuffle forward, jumping down Dad's tummy, making him groan some more.

I pushed myself forward one more time. Except that maybe I pushed a bit too hard because I thumped into the back of Charlie, grabbing him round his waist because I was too far from the handles to hold on any more.

'Harry!' he shouted. 'Stop bumping me! I slipping!'

He was right, he was slipping. And he wasn't the only one either. Dad's knees were trying to squash us to stop us sliding away but the mat underneath us was moving, too.

'Hold on, Charlie!' shouted Dad. 'We're not ready!'

'I *am* holding on!' shouted back Charlie.

Have I explained this properly to you? Dad's holding onto the bars, trying to get comfy on the mat. I'm sat between his legs, holding onto Charlie. And Charlie is now sat on my lap, holding onto the ends of Dad's shorts. And all the time massive jets of water are trying to push us down the slide.

Now when Charlie grabs hold of something, you can't make him let go. It doesn't matter if it's your hand, a packet of mini Cheddars or – in this case – Dad's shorts. But Dad's shorts weren't so grabby. In fact, they gave up completely.

'Whoooooaaah!' said Charlie, and it was the right noise because we were off down the slide! Charlie, me, the mat and… Dad's shorts. Without Dad in them.

Looking back I could see him still grabbing onto the metal bar, stretched out on his back with no clothes on, jets of water spraying all over him.

He let go with one hand and tried to make some hand pants with the other, but it was too late: the people in the queue were already howling with laughter and pointing at him.

And that's all I saw because Charlie and I were off! We zoomed into the tunnel and round the first bend, sliding up the walls, screaming like mad. After that it just got faster and more terrifying. We went round in a complete circle at one point. I think we might even have done a loop-the-loop.

But you know what was funny? At the top we were screaming because we were frightened. But by the bottom, when we plopped into the pool, we were screaming with laughter. Same noise, different feeling.

We plopped into the pool and bobbed up, coughing and spluttering. Mum was waiting with the towels at the shallow end.

A quick rub down and Charlie was off again.

'Don't go too far, Charlie!' said Mum as he waddled away.

It was only then that we noticed the crowds of people by the side of the pool, all pointing up at the top of the slide. They were the same people who had been so angry when Charlie had mixed

up their stuff.

But they weren't angry now. They were laughing, shouting, and taking pictures with their phones… of Dad. Because Dad was still up there, hanging on.

He'd somehow managed to grab another mat and he was trying to wrap it around him like a towel. Except the water kept pushing it sideways and unrolling it and he only had one hand to hold it.

As we watched, he lost his grip on the mat and it zipped off down the slide. He let go of the bar, covered himself up with his hands and followed the mat into the tunnel.

You could see his shadow as he went round the bends; we all followed him round and round, down and down, until he shot out at the bottom, feet first, still absolutely naked, into the pool.

Everyone – and I mean *everyone* – cheered.

'Smile for the camera!' shouted a man.

'I got you on YouTube!' shouted a boy waving a phone.

'Nice bum!' shouted a woman nearby. Mum turned and gave her a funny look.

Dad swam to the side and waved at Mum to

bring a towel. She smiled and pointed to the steps. Dad looked very grumpy and waved again, so Mum took a towel down. With a final flash of his white bottom, Dad was up on the side and wrapped up.

Back by the sun loungers everyone calmed down and Dad started to smile again.

'I'm glad I gave everyone a treat, anyway. Where are my shorts?' he said.

'Harry had them,' said Mum.

'No I didn't,' I said, 'Charlie did.'

'Charlie?'

Charlie was back.

He stood and pointed.

There, at the end of the tube and pulled over the head of The Dragon, were Dad's baggy, soggy shorts.

'I might have known. Cheeky Charlie,' sighed Dad, and he plodded off to get them, wrapped carefully in his towel.

Christmas Fair

'It's still wonky,' I said. 'And you've forgotten the big star on the top.'

Dad was putting up the Christmas tree and wasn't doing a very good job. Charlie wasn't helping either: he took the shiny baubles from the box, put them down his trousers and danced around to the Christmas music until they rolled out by his shoes.

'Where's that star gone, then?' asked Dad. 'We had it last year.'

I looked at Charlie. Charlie looked at me with the funny face he uses when he's spilt his drink, broken something, or done a poo.

'That reminds me,' Dad said, with a serious look. 'Did you know your grandad was a thief?'

'A thief?' I said. 'Really? Which grandad? Did

he go to prison?'

Mum, who was making some gingerbread biscuits for the tree, looked up.

'Don't fall for it, Harry.'

'I'm talking about your mum's dad,' whispered Dad, 'Grandad Lou. He stole the stars from the sky, and he put them in your Mummy's eyes.'

Mum groaned, loudly.

'How can you steal the stars? What does that even mean?' I said to Dad.

He sighed. 'Never mind. My wit is wasted on this family. Now bring me that grubby fairy with the missing leg, maybe we'll shove her on top instead… ah, Charlie! You've got the star. I might have known.'

My little brother pulled the star out from under his jumper and at last the tree was done.

I fetched my letter to Santa which I had nearly finished, and put it under the tree. It's tricky, isn't it, deciding what you want. Here's what it said:

Dear Father Chrismas
I have been an extreemly good girl. Please give me a bike, some new pens, a bag and

(Then I'd left a big space. Really big, about as big as my pencil case, so I could fill in some extra stuff later, when I thought of it.)

Lots of love
Harriet xxxxx

Charlie saw me and ran into the lounge to fetch his letter too, shouting 'Farmer Christmas! Farmer Christmas!' He's so silly.

Because he can't write, Mum had given him a magazine and some glue. He'd ripped out pictures of the things he wanted for Christmas and stuck them to a piece of paper. Here's what he chose:

☆ A bottle of perfume
☆ A ship
☆ A snowy mountain
☆ A lady's bottom wearing some funny pants
☆ A mobile phone, just like Dad's.

Can you imagine Santa trying to get down the chimney with a lady's bottom in his sack?

'Right,' said Mum. 'These biscuits are done. Let's go to the fair.'

Do you have fairs at your school? They're brilliant, aren't they? You get to go into loads of classrooms, even the Year 6 ones. I once went into the staffroom, too. You can decorate biscuits, win jars of sweets and even run in the corridors.

It was busy. I mean really, really busy. The noise in the hall was a bit scary at first. If we made that much noise in assembly it would make Mr Bartlett – that's our head teacher – so mad his head would pop. There were grown-ups everywhere, sitting on children's chairs and talking, and children running around between them.

It was nearly lunchtime. We zig-zagged our way to the hatch where I normally get my baked potato-if-I-have-a-blue-band, or pasta-if-I-have-a-yellow-band. But I never wear a green band because I don't like vegetables except broccoli and sometimes peas.

This time though, they were selling massive sausage rolls. Why don't we get those for school dinner? It's not fair. Anyway, Mum bought one for everyone and we made our way to an empty table that Dad had found, saying 'excuse me excuse me excuse me' all the way.

The sausage rolls were *scrumdiddlyumptious* (I

learned that word in carpet time last week). As I was munching mine, I noticed that Charlie, standing at the end of the table, was nibbling all the pastry off the outside – just like I do with the chocolate on KitKats. He saw me watching him.

'Is for later,' he said quietly.

Sure enough, when he had finished he took the huge, wobbly pink bar of sausage meat – still with little bits of white pastry stuck to it – and put it down the back of his trousers!

'I got no pockets,' he explained.

But just as he was finishing his sentence, Dad came up behind him.

'Let's get you sat down properly, little one,' he said before lifting him by the armpits.

'No Daddeeeeeee!' I shouted, but it was too late. Flumph! He plopped Charlie down onto one of the chairs.

Tears started rolling down Charlie's cheeks.

'What on earth is the matter?' said Mum crossly.

Charlie reached down his trousers and pulled out a handful of squished pink sausage meat.

Mum let out a little yelp, the kind of noise that my cousin's dog makes if you tread on his paw by accident. Everyone on the other tables turned to see what was going on.

A bit later, after I'd explained and Mum had taken Charlie to the toilet to scrape the lunch off his bottom, we went exploring.

'Can I go on my own?' I asked.

'Yes, but you'll need to take Charlie with you,' said Mum. 'Make sure he doesn't leave the hall or get into trouble.'

Well. I don't know if you've ever tried to look after a 3-year-old but it's boring. And impossible. They run off, they squeeze into tiny gaps, they stop you talking to your friend Delilah. That's what Charlie did. So I thought, well I'll just tell Delilah what I'm getting for Christmas, then I'll find Mum and tell her that Charlie is lost.

I was just showing Delilah my new rainbow bracelet when I heard someone shouting. Then another voice, then a woman screaming, a proper *that shouldn't happen* scream.

I looked across to where all the noise was coming from, near the Christmas tree in the corner. At first I couldn't see what was happening: lots of people were pointing at the wall. But then I spotted… well, can you imagine who it was?

Yep, Charlie. But he wasn't where you'd expect. You see the walls of our hall have bars on them that the older children use for climbing during PE. And Charlie is a good climber – a very good climber. In fact he'd got right to the top, higher than I've ever seen, up near the ceiling.

And it gets worse: he was only holding on with one chubby hand. The other? That was reaching out towards the star on the top of the Christmas tree.

And what was everyone else doing? That's a good question. All these grown-ups, the people who are always telling me what to do, were standing there, looking and pointing. Several of them had their mouths open, and I could even see what they were eating. Yuck.

But it didn't last long because quick as a flash, the Year 3 teacher Mrs Buckle raced up the bars to reach him. It was amazing because Mrs Buckle is quite *plump* (I hope that's the right word to use because she's lovely). I've never even seen her walk quickly but here she was, climbing the bars like a chubby monkey wearing a flowery dress. Awesome.

She was just in time because Charlie couldn't hold on any longer. He kind-of-fell, kind-of-slid

down on top of her; she grabbed him with one arm and pressed him into her chest. And Mrs Buckle has a very big chest. He almost disappeared.

Finally, two dads climbed up besides her to try and help. But Mrs Buckle climbed down all on her own.

Suddenly everyone was cheering, shouting and clapping, and someone even did a big whistle. Mum hugged Charlie and I squeezed through to join them.

'Are you OK?' asked Mum, but Charlie was crying too much to reply.

Now I'm pretty sure that if I climbed the bars, Mum would be really, really cross. But as you should know by now, normal rules don't apply to Charlie. Instead, Mum picked him up and gave him lots of cuddles. It's crazy, I tell you.

WAIT A MINUTE.

You maybe need to stop reading. Because to tell the rest of this story about Charlie, I need to explain all about Father Christmas. And I mean *everything*. So if you are six or something like that, you need your Mum or Dad to say it's OK for you to finish the story.

Have you checked it's OK? Good. That means you're old enough to know the secret – maybe you already do. But I have to be careful because my Mum always stops me when I talk about this at home, saying I must not 'spoil the surprise' for Charlie.

So here we go. Here's an easy question. Do you think that the blow-up Santa that shops have in the window is real? Of course not, it's just a toy. Charlie thinks it is, but that's because he's three.

Here's a harder question. If you wore a Father Christmas outfit, would that make you Father Christmas? No, of course not! That's just dressing up. You knew that, didn't you?

And now the last question, I promise. When you see Santa on the telly, or in the shopping centre or the supermarket, is it always the *real* Father Christmas? If you think it is, you should stop reading NOW!

But if you know it isn't always the real Father

Christmas then you're really clever like me. You're probably eight, or even more. And you're definitely a girl. Or maybe a very clever boy.

Because clever children like us know that even if it's just a make-believe Father Christmas you have to pretend it's the real one. That way you'll still get a good present – but of course it won't be on your list, because only the real Father Christmas has that.

So that's what I was doing as we went into see him. The teachers had turned Miss White's office into a grotto with spray snow on the windows and fairy lights round the door. And guarding that door was Mrs Wood, the Year 5 teacher; she was dressed up like an elf, although I've never seen an elf drinking tea and eating biscuits before.

It was our turn. Mrs Wood took me and Charlie by the hand and led us into the office. There was Father Christmas, waiting for us. He looked real. He even sounded real. But I spotted a few clues.

CLUE 1: he was wearing glasses, but not just any glasses: these had *Red or Dead* written on the side, just like the ones that Ellie's dad wears: I'd noticed it because that's a funny thing to have on your glasses. Although maybe not for Father

Christmas. Perhaps Father Christmas goes to the same shop as Ellie's dad.

CLUE TWO: his bag, tucked behind his chair. Not his sack of presents: that was next to the door, behind the tea-drinking elf. This was his private bag and it was bright yellow with green writing, just like the one that Ellie's dad carries to the train station in the morning. Hmm.

Charlie was telling Santa that he wanted a ship and some perfume for Christmas. While they talked I noticed **CLUE 3**: Santa's bag was open and full of his stuff. I could see a lunchbox with some sandwiches in it, a mobile phone, and

something else, too: a car magazine. **CLUE 4**.

Would the real Santa be interested in cars? No! You can't drive a normal car on snow. If it was a magazine about reindeers, or presents, then maybe. But it wasn't. There was no way this was the real Santa.

But I pretended not to see, and then Charlie and I swapped chairs. Santa asked me if I'd been a good girl. I said yes, of course. He asked me if I was looking forward to Christmas. I said yes, of course. And he asked me what I wanted to get and I told him a bike.

And then it was over. Charlie, who was crawling around on the floor, jumped up and ran to Mrs Wood, who gave us both a present. Mine was way too small to be a bike.

'Charlie, you're not supposed to unwrap your present!' I said.

'Oh Charlie,' said Mum. 'Go on then Harry, open yours if you want.'

I did want. Charlie got a packet of coloured pencils and he looked quite grumpy about it. I felt happy just because I didn't get any: coloured pencils are rubbish, they never work properly. I don't even know why they exist.

I got a Dora pencil case, which was quite nice actually.

Next stop: the secret present room. This one is brilliant: it's just for children, no grown-ups allowed. Mum gave us 50p each. Charlie and I went in.

Inside was even busier than the hall. There were lots of children wrapping up presents and a few grown-ups to help. We squeezed into spaces at the wrapping desks and I handed over my 50p. I got a bottle of pink bubble bath, which will be perfect for Mum.

It took me ages to wrap it but Charlie took even longer: I heard him telling the grown-ups to 'go away'. How rude. And when we came out, Charlie had two presents... and still had his 50p! The presents were really badly wrapped with lots and lots of Sellotape going all the way around.

'Who are they for?' asked Mum.

'Is for Harry, and is for me,' said Charlie.

'Oh thank you Charlie!' I said. 'Can I open it now?'

'Not now,' said Mum. 'Let's just put those away for later,' and she put them in her bag. Boo.

Next stop was the 'Win a bottle' room. Dad had turned up again, but by now the fair was nearly over and there wasn't much left. I picked three tickets for Mum and Charlie did the same for Dad. If the number on your ticket ended in a 5 or a 0 then you won the prize with the same number on the table.

We opened mine first: only one of the three was a winner, and Dad got a bottle of apple juice. He made a face at me because he wanted the wine.

Charlie's turn. He handed Dad his first ticket: it was a winner. The helper looked at the table but there was nothing on the matching spot, so she gave him a bottle of beer from behind the desk. Big smile from Dad.

Ticket number two was another winner. But again, there was nothing on the matching spot. The helper frowned, but again she gave Dad a bottle from behind the desk: more beer. An even bigger smile from Dad.

Ticket number three was another winner!

'You really are my lucky little elf, Charlie,' said Dad, patting him on the head as he waited for the helper. She was talking to the other grown-up – Mr Jones, the deputy head teacher.

'Can I just see what's in your hand?' said Mr Jones, bending down to Charlie.

Charlie grinned, and opened his podgy fist to reveal hundreds of tickets, all scrumpled up.

'Charlie, where did you get all those?' asked Dad.

Charlie pointed at the bin behind the bottle table. The same bin where the helper had been putting all the winning tickets.

'And where are the three tickets you chose?' continued Dad, sounding a bit sad now.

Charlie lifted his foot.

'Ah,' said Dad, putting his bottles of beer back on the table. 'Slight problem. Sorry about that. You'll want these back, I think. Time to head home.'

He pushed us all out of the room: I think he was worried that Mr Jones would call the police because Charlie had cheated.

The fair was over. We shuffled out slowly. Guess who I saw through the staffroom window? Father Christmas! He was talking to Mr Bartlett, and he looked really cross. Like I said, I'm pretty certain it wasn't the real Santa. I don't think Santa gets cross.

'OK, all set?' Dad said, starting the car engine. 'Jingle Bells' started playing. Now in our car, when the engine starts, the radio often comes on and that's what I thought it was.

Charlie thought so too. 'Bingle Jells, Bingle Jells, Bingle awwl the way!' he sang.

But the music stopped. And then started again.

'Where is that hideous tune coming from?' asked Dad.

'I don't know, it sounds like something in the back,' said Mum.

'Take a look, will you,' said Dad. 'I've got my seatbelt on.' Mum sighed and got out.

'It's getting louder!' I shouted as Mum moved stuff around in the boot.

'It's something in the pushchair,' she said, rummaging around. 'It's this present!' She held up the one that Charlie had wrapped for himself. 'Charlie, what have you got here?'

'No no no no no!' cried Charlie as Mum unwrapped it.

'But seriously, Charlie, this is a mobile phone!' said Mum, pulling it out of the Sellotape. 'Where on earth did you get this?'

Charlie said nothing and looked at his feet.

'That's a new iPhone – someone will be missing that,' said Dad. 'Just answer it, love, you'll find out soon enough.'

'Umm, hello?' said Mum. I didn't know who it was, but I could hear they were quite angry. 'Oh hello, it's Harry's mum here. Yes it is, I'm not quite sure how we've ended up with it, but I think it might have been something to do with Charlie... I'm so sorry,' she said. 'Of course, I'll drop it round on the way home. I really am very sorry.'

She put the phone into her pocket.

'Who was it Mum?'

'Charlie knows who's phone it is, don't you Charlie?'

Charlie sniffed. In a very small voice he whispered, 'Is Farmer Christmas phone.'

'No, seriously?' said Dad. 'You took Santa's mobile? From his grotto? I don't know if I should laugh or drop you off at the prison!'

And that, it seemed, was that.

'Ellie's dad will find a way to get it back to Santa,' said Mum. I think we know the truth about my school Father Christmas, don't we?

Charlie was still sniffing and Dad was still chuckling. 'Nicked Santa's phone... just wait until I see him on the train,' said Dad. 'Charlie, it may be Christmas, but you are bad for my elf. Bad for my elf, do you get it? Elf, get it? Sounds like health? Elf?'

Everyone in the car was silent.

'Ah, never mind,' said Dad, and started the engine. 'I don't know why I bother.'

PS I almost forgot: can you guess what was in my present from Charlie? It was those coloured pencils. They're rubbish... but you knew that, didn't you?

Soft Play

It was the really boring week just after Christmas, the worst one in the world when you can't go out because it's raining and you don't want to stay in because everyone is so annoying. Charlie was running around shouting nonsense, Mum was shouting at Charlie and Dad said he was doing 'something important' on the computer.

'I'm bored,' I said to Mum.

'All aboard!' shouted Charlie, and he made a whistling noise like a train.

Mum turned to me. 'You know what they say, Harry, only boring people get...'

'...bored, yes I know, you always say that!' I replied.

'Say dat! Say dat! Say dat!' chanted Charlie, marching up and down the hall, waving his arms and stomping his feet.

'Can we go to the park?' I asked, but I knew the answer already because I could hear the rain gurgling out of the drainpipe by the front door.

'Not a chance,' said Mum, 'but I suppose we could go to Our Space, if you want?'

'Yay!' I shouted.

'Outer space! Outer space! Outer space!' shouted Charlie.

Our Space – or Outer Space as Charlie likes to call it – is the soft play place near us. Have you got one of those near you? Does it have a bumpy slide, and a curly wurly one too that's all dark and scary? I go down them on my own now. It's brilliant.

So I put my shoes on, Mum changed Charlie's nappy and shoved it into the stinky bag in the hall, and we got ready to go. It always takes ages with people running in and out of the front door, putting stuff in the car and shouting at each other.

'Seriously love, what do you keep in this change bag?' said Dad. 'It weighs a ton.'

'Just the essentials,' said Mum. 'Now come on, let's go before it's too late.'

We left at last. I don't know why grown-ups make such a fuss.

When we got there it was really noisy: a girl was having a Disney Princess birthday party in the side room and girls kept running in and out. Most of them had long blonde flicky hair and they were all wearing pink party t-shirts.

One of the mums came out and shouted out that the balloon man had arrived. The girls in the pink t-shirts ran inside.

'Are those people made of money?' muttered Mum as we wiggled through the tables.

'I think it looks brilliant,' I said. 'I wish I was invited.'

'Rubbish,' replied Mum. 'Your party in the park was much better. You played hide and seek, remember?'

Mum seriously thinks that hide and seek was better than a princess party at Our Space. I don't think so!

We put the bags down at a spare table and immediately Charlie ran off.

'Charlie! Don't go too... ' Mum started to say. 'Oh well, I'm sure he'll be fine. Keep an eye out for him will you Harry? Who knows where he'll end up.'

Well I had better things to do than chase around

looking for Charlie. I wandered over and sat on the baby climbing frame, just outside the party room. I could hear all the girls inside, laughing and giggling. They were giggling a lot, in fact: the balloon man must have been really funny. I wished I was at the party.

OK, this was weird, now they were shouting. And one of them was screaming.

The door opened. A mum stood with her hand on hips, her face bright pink like the girls' t-shirts.

'It's time you went back to your parents, wherever they are,' she said crossly, in a really posh voice. 'And put those presents down.'

Behind her, I could just make out the face of her uninvited guest – it was Charlie, of course. He was hard to see because his top half was hidden behind an armful of things: face paint kits, colouring books, some clothes, even a robot dog. Meanwhile his bottom half was

mostly covered up by a mountain of wrapping paper, all torn and crumpled.

'Seriously, put those things down immediately, before I call for your mummy,' said the posh woman.

For once, Charlie did as he was told. But because it was Charlie, he just opened his arms wide and all the presents fell into the pile of wrapping paper with a giant clatter. He stepped carefully over the pile and walked out of the room with a cheeky smile.

Charlie ran straight past me so I walked to the climbing equipment for big children. I clambered right to the very top – you have to go through the ball pit, up the main tower, across the rope bridge and up the little tower next to the bumpy slide.

From there I could see everything: Mum was sat at the table, playing with her phone; Dad was buying coffee and hopefully a snack for me, too; and Charlie… well he was around somewhere. Probably causing trouble again.

Ah, there he was, coming my way. Except he was walking really weirdly, sideways like a crab, dragging the change bag behind him. He really is quite a strange boy. Do you have a brother? I hope that if you do he's a bit strange too, because then you'll know how I feel.

I whizzed down the bumpy slide, glad that I was wearing my slippy-slidey leggings. It was getting busier so it took me ages to get back to Mum who gave me a finger of Kit Kat. I waved at Charlie but he was half-way up the tower and wasn't looking.

'Where's the change bag?' asked Mum.

Dad didn't answer, and I carried on trying to bite all the chocolate off my Kit Kat finger without nibbling the wafer bit.

'No but seriously, where is it?' she said.

'I think I saw Charlie with it,' I said. A bit of chocolate fell to the floor but I picked it up quickly.

'Why would Charlie have the change bag?' asked Mum, 'and where is he, anyway?'

'I saw him over there,' I said, and pointed towards the entrance by the tower where a crowd of children were standing around one of the Our Space helpers.

Lots of the children were laughing and pointing up, but the woman looked 'a bit shirty', which is what my Mum says when Dad is a bit grumpy.

Then I saw what the children were pointing at. Or who they were pointing at, because it was

Charlie. He was standing at the top of the tower wearing a 'nappy hat'. You do know what one of those is, don't you? It's when you get a clean nappy and put it on your head. You should try it, it's really funny. Just make sure it hasn't got poo in it otherwise you'll get it stuck in your hair.

But there was another reason why the children were pointing and laughing. As we watched, Charlie reached into the change bag by his feet and pulled out another nappy... except this one wasn't clean. It was all rolled up into a ball, like the smelly ones that Dad throws down the stairs.

With a big grin on his face, Charlie did a little run and threw the nappy ball down the curly wurly slide. A few seconds later the children cheered as it came shooting out of the bottom and landed in the ball pool.

I'll tell you one person who wasn't cheering: the Our Space woman. She was too busy climbing up the tower, chased by Mum who had run across and was catching up, three rungs at a time. Brilliant, they were having a race!

'Come on Mummy!' I shouted, but it was no good: the Our Space woman got to the top first. It wasn't fair, she had a head start.

A bit later, when Charlie had come down with Mum and Dad had finished getting a bit shirty with the Our Space woman, Mum decided it was time to leave anyway and we all got into the car.

As we went round the roundabout, Charlie did what he always does and shouted 'Old Macdonald's!' as soon as he saw the McDonald's clown. Only this time you could hardly hear him speak and he covered me in a spray of crumbs.

'Charlie, what are you eating?' said Mum, turning around.

'Cake from my party bag,' said Charlie, holding up a pink Disney Princess bag and looking extremely pleased with himself.

'Oh Charlie,' said Dad, who was driving. 'You really are a very naughty, very cheeky boy. Now give me a bit of that cake.'

And he winked at Charlie in the mirror.

Hospital

When my Dad was a little boy, his mummy died. Well, he wasn't *really* little. He says he was a teenager, so quite big actually. He says his mummy got a poorly tummy and then she went to hospital and then she died.

I think maybe I should feel sad about that, but I don't because I never met her. If I look at the old photo of her on the landing I can make myself feel a bit sad, but not enough to cry. So I just make a sad face and say 'Awww' and give Dad a cuddle to make him feel better.

But Granny Fran, my Mum's mummy, is still really alive, even though she's very, very old. She's 143 or something like that, but she can still walk and talk and do the shopping. But she's not very good at jumping sideways, which is what she should have done when the car went across the zebra crossing and bonked her on the leg.

She fell over and an ambulance came and took her to hospital.

'Did it have its nee-naws on, Granny?' I asked her afterwards.

'I don't know, dear. Yes, I think it did.'

'Cool,' I said, and Charlie ran up and down the room shouting 'NEE NAW NEE NAW!' until Mum told him to 'put a sock in it', which was a

silly thing to say because then Charlie started to eat his socks.

Anyway, we didn't find out about Granny's accident until Mum took Charlie and me to see her in the hospital after school.

'Is she going to die?' asked Charlie.

'Don't be stupid, the car only hit her on the leg,' I said, although I wasn't sure. After all, Dad's mummy only had a tummy ache when she went to hospital.

'We don't say 'stupid' thank you, Harry,' said Mum, 'and no, she's not going to die. She was very lucky. She's just a bit shaken up, that's all.'

Being hit by a car didn't sound lucky to me – even if it did just shake you up – but I stayed quiet. Soon we were walking up and down long hospital corridors, getting in and out of lifts, trying to find Granny.

Eventually we came to some big doors with a sign above them that I couldn't read. I asked Mum what it said.

'Geriatrics,' said Mum. 'That means medicine for old people.'

'Jerry tricks?' shouted Charlie. 'I love tricks. I want see Jerry. What tricks does Jerry do? Is he poorly? Can we see him now? Can he do balloon swords? Can he turn into a giraffe? Will I... '

'Enough, Charlie,' said Mum. 'Let's go and see Granny.'

Through the doors was a big desk with loads of nurses chatting behind it. While Mum spoke to one of them, several of the others crowded around Charlie, ruffling his hair and generally making a fuss. As usual.

The head nurse told Mum that Mrs Whitfield – that's my Granny's grown-up name – was in a private room at the end of the ward so we dragged Charlie away from his fan club and off we went.

There were a lot of old people. Some were propped up on pillows, smiling; some had visitors, including children who were mostly playing on phones. One old man near the end was snoring like a gruffalo. He had a hairy white chin, crazy, flyaway hair and blue pyjamas with the collar sticking up. Charlie went up to get a better look because every time he snored his lips wobbled and his head did a little waggle.

Suddenly, he stopped snoring. Completely. He was totally silent, and very still. Charlie crept closer. 'Is he dead?' he said loudly, stepping right up to the bed. He reached out his chubby hand to touch the man's arm.

'Boo!' shouted the man, his eyes flicking open. 'I'm not dead yet, little'un! These lovely nurses are keeping me alive,' he said, pointing at one of them. She rolled her eyes.

'Ah ha ha!' shouted Charlie. Instead of being frightened like me, he found it funny. 'Ah ha ha ha ha! He's a funny man! He play tricks!'

Charlie ran to Mum who had come back to find us. 'I found Jerry!' he said. 'Watch, he do tricks!'

'Leave the poor man alone,' said Mum, although the man didn't seem to mind at all; he just winked at Charlie, and closed his eyes.

We found Granny in a room at the end of the ward.

'What are you doing in here, Granny?' I asked. 'Don't you like the other people?'

'It's not that, dear,' said Granny, who was sat up in bed. 'The nurses just thought I could do with a bit more rest, that's all.'

'And you get your own telly,' I pointed out,

though it was switched off. Boring.

Charlie started to explore the room, though there wasn't much to explore. Just a couple of armchairs and a table on this side of the bed. He disappeared around the other side.

'Where's that cheeky brother of yours gone?' said Granny, but she didn't have to wait long for an answer because suddenly there was a whining, clicking noise and Granny's bed started to lift up into the air.

'Charlie,' she said calmly as she went higher and higher, 'you shouldn't be playing with those buttons.'

'Sorry,' said a voice from under the bed and the whining noise stopped. Then it started again, and Granny's bed started to sink down.

'Charlie!' said Mum sharply.

'But I just putting it back!' he protested, his head popping up. Mum couldn't argue with that.

One of the nurses put her head around the door. 'Have you chosen your lunch yet Mrs W?'

'No, not yet, dear,' said Granny. 'I was just playing with my grandson. Give me a minute.'

'Aah, bless. He looks like a right cutie,' said the nurse. 'I'll come back in a minute then.'

'What's she talking about?' I asked.

'This,' said Granny, holding out a piece of paper. 'It's how we choose our meals. You tell me what's on the menu, Harriet.'

I read it out. 'For starters you can have carrot soup...'

'Yuck!' shouted Charlie from under the bed.

'...or a melon boat,' I continued. 'A melon boat? Weird. What's that?'

'Lemon yuck boat cool,' said Charlie, who was now peering into Mum's handbag.

'It's nowhere near as exciting as it sounds, dear,' said Granny. 'Like most of the food here, I'm afraid. I can't wait to get home.'

'There's cottage pie or cauliflower cheese after that,' I read, 'then treacle sponge and custard for pudding.'

'Cottages yuck flowers yuck custard yuck,' muttered Charlie into Mum's bag. We ignored him.

'Tick the melon and the cottage pie for me please, Harriet,' said Granny, 'and then Charlie, can I trust you to take it to a nurse for me?'

'Yay!' said Charlie, who loves being given jobs to do. He hopped from one foot to the other in excitement while I ticked the boxes and carefully wrote 'Mrs Witfield' on the top. Charlie grabbed the menu and disappeared out of the door.

While he was gone, I told Granny about school, Mum told her that Charlie still wasn't out of nappies yet, and Granny said he was a bit old for that now, and maybe Mum should be a bit more strict. I said I thought that was a good idea, too.

After we'd been talking for ages, Mum asked me to go and find Charlie. Back out on the ward I couldn't see him anywhere.

'Can I help you?' said a nurse behind the desk.

'I'm looking for my brother,' I said. 'Mum sent him with the lunch menu but he hasn't come back.'

'Is he the cute little chappy with the curly hair?' she asked.

'He's definitely not cute, but he's certainly curly, so that's probably him,' I said.

'In that case, I have a good idea where he might be,' she said, and she took me by the hand and we walked down the ward. Everyone was looking at

106

me and smiling. I think I want to be a nurse when I grow up.

'He brought us the menu but he'd made a few changes,' she said, pulling a menu slip out of her pocket and handing it to me.

It was the same menu but my tick marks had been scribbled out. And in the space next to them Charlie had drawn a wobbly picture of a green triple-decker burger. And some green chips.

I turned to the nurse. 'My brother is so dumb,' I said. 'Now Granny will miss her lunch!'

'Don't worry, I've sorted it,' said the nurse. 'No harm done. Now then, he definitely toddled off this way… but he might just have turned in here,' she said, pointing at a door with a sign on it that said *TV Lounge*.

The room was full of high-backed pink chairs, all turned to face the TV in the corner which was showing a crazy cartoon. You could see a few tufts of white hair over the tops of the chairs, so I knew there were people watching. But there was something else, too: the sound of chuntering.

Do you know what chuntering is? It's what Charlie does when he's complaining about something he wants but he can't have. There's lots of things he wants but he can't have, so he does a lot of chuntering: when he asks for a ham and jelly baby sandwich, or a cloud for his birthday, or a gingerbread man instead of his teddy at bedtime.

But this chuntering was the sound of unhappy grown-ups.

'What's going on here then, Grace?' my friendly nurse asked a wrinkly old lady.

'I think there's something wrong with the telly,' she said, winking at me.

'Get it off!' someone shouted from near the front. 'I want *Countdown* back on!'

'This is a rubbish programme! Someone call a nurse!' said another.

'Where has that little lad gone with the remote control?' said a third.

Ah. I knew what was going on here.

I turned around. I'm an expert Charlie-spotter now. I just think, 'Where would Charlie hide?' and I'm usually right. In this case I could see a low wall next to an emergency exit and chairs pushed up against it.

'Shh,' I said to the nurse. 'Follow me.'

The nurse started to do that funny tiptoe walk that they always do on *Scooby-Doo* whenever they want to be really quiet. I've never seen a grown-up do that before.

The nurse and I crept around the back of the chairs, crouched down, and slowly put our heads around the partition.

There, in the small space behind the chair but with a brilliant view of the telly, sat Charlie. But you'll never believe this, because he had a friend! Next to him, separated only by a huge bag of crisps and the remote control, sat the old man in the blue pyjamas. Both of them were pushing big handfuls into their mouths, bits dropping everywhere.

The old man saw us. 'Looks like we've been rumbled, Charlie boy,' he said with a smile.

'Mr Jamieson,' said the nurse calmly, 'I hate to interrupt your tea party, but this little chap is wanted by his mother. And you're not supposed to be out of bed, either.'

'What do you think, Charlie?' he asked. 'Shall we give ourselves up?'

Charlie looked at Mr Jamieson and nodded. 'Dey found us,' Charlie said. He picked up the crisps and together they crawled out of their hiding place. Charlie sprang to his feet, but Mr Jamieson had to be helped up by the nurse, and it took ages.

'Come on, Charlie,' said the nurse, taking his hand. But Charlie shook it off and took the old man's hand instead. Carefully and slowly, Charlie led him back across the room, threading his way between the chairs, ignoring all the chuntering grown-ups. The nurse and I followed.

As they reached the door, the nurse held out her hand. 'Umm Charlie, haven't you forgotten something?'

Charlie gave the old man his crisps and pulled the remote control out of his trousers. He handed it back to the nurse without a word.

'Nice try, soldier,' said Mr Jamieson. 'You can't win 'em all.'

'Goodness, what a cheeky boy you are,' said the nurse, but she smiled, and opened the door back to the hospital ward.

THE END

Read on...for free!

For children: so did you enjoy my stories? If you did, that awesome Cheeky Charlie Mini-Book is waiting for you – completely free!

It's all about me and Charlie at a music festival. Expect smelly toilets and a man with incredibly hairy feet. It's a humdinger, which is another Dad word for excellent, and he's still right.

So find a grown-up, get them to read the bit underneath. Don't wait!

Adults: I sometimes send out emails about new Charlie stories that are about to be published, other books that I'm working on, and stuff I think you'll like. I don't do it often, and I try to make them as useful as possible. Sometimes even funny. As a thank you, I'll send you *Festival* – a seven-chapter Charlie Mini-book. It's packed with fun and it'll do enough bedtimes to last until the weekend. After that, I'm afraid you're on your own.

Sound good? To get it, just sign up for my emails at **matwaugh.co.uk/freebook** now.

One last thing...

Readers: have you ever bought something rubbish online?

I have. Recently I bought a bath panel that wasn't waterproof, a 'silent' extractor fan that whirs like a tornado while I'm on the toilet, and an iPhone holder that snapped like spaghetti.

Serves me right, I didn't read the reviews.

Reviews matter. And *your* Amazon review matters to me – and influences other readers, too.

Just give it a star rating. Leave a word or a sentence. Use your real name, your initials or 'Mr Whippy'. (Maybe not that last one). In return you'll get my gratitude, instant karma and everlasting life, or at least one of the above.

Thank you in advance and see you next time!

Mat

PS You may also be eligible to get new Charlie stories first and free. Sign up at **matwaugh.co.uk/ freebook**

About Mat Waugh

I'm a father of three young girls. I'm often tired. These two things are connected.

I live in Tunbridge Wells, which is a lively, lovely town in the south east of England.

When I was seven I wrote to Clive King. He's the author of my favourite childhood book, *Stig of the Dump*, which is about a caveman who lives in a house made out of rubbish. I asked Clive if there was going to be a sequel, but he said no.

I've had lots of writing and editing jobs, but mostly for other people.

I forgot: I also had a crazy year when I thought I wanted to be a teacher. But then I found out how hard teachers work, and that you have to buy your own biscuits. So I stopped, and now I just visit schools to eat theirs.

I always wanted to write my own stories, but I could never find the right moment. So I waited until I had children and had no spare time at all.

Finally, I love hearing from readers. If that's you, then you can email me: *mail@matwaugh.co.uk* – just ask your parents first.

Also by Mat Waugh

Cheeky Charlie: Bugs and Bananas (Book 2)
Cheeky Charlie: King of Chaos (Book 3)
Cheeky Charlie: He Didn't Mean It (Book 4)
Cheeky Charlie: Who Did That? (Book 5)
Cheeky Charlie: Out of Bounds (Book 6)

Cheeky Charlie: Festival
Join my email list and get a free Charlie eBook.
matwaugh.co.uk/freebook

The Fun Factor: for kids 8 to 12
In a remote village, the stuff everyone loves is disappearing by the day. First to go is the internet. Next up: phones, pizzas, TV channels and even the dishwasher. Twelve-year-old Thora and her friends struggle to see what's so fun about the good old days, but soon discover they're guinea pigs in a decidedly high-tech social experiment…

Awesome Jokes: for kids aged 5 up
Fantastic Wordsearches: for kids aged 6 up
What's the Magic Word? for kids 3 to 5

Made in United States
North Haven, CT
30 April 2022